Curious Case of the
Ransom Riddler

By Kyla Steinkraus
Illustrated by David Ouro

Rourke
Educational Media
rourkeeducationalmedia.com

www.rourkeeducationalmedia.com

Edited by: Keli Sipperley
Cover layout by: Renee Brady
Interior layout by: Jen Thomas
Cover and Interior Illustrations by: David Ouro

Library of Congress PCN Data

Curious Case of the Ransom Riddler / Kyla Steinkraus
(Rourke's Mystery Chapter Books)
ISBN (hard cover)(alk. paper) 978-1-63430-382-8
ISBN (soft cover) 978-1-63430-482-5
ISBN (e-Book) 978-1-63430-577-8
Library of Congress Control Number: 2015933738

Printed in the United States of America, North Mankato, Minnesota

Dear Parents and Teachers:

With twists and turns and red herrings, readers will enjoy the challenge of Rourke's Mystery Chapter Books. This series set at Watson Elementary School builds a cast of characters that readers quickly feel connected to. Embedded in each mystery are experiences that readers encounter at home or school. Topics of friendship, family, and growing up are featured within each book.

Mysteries open many doors for young readers and turn them into lifelong readers because they can't wait to find out what happens next. Readers build comprehension strategies by searching out clues through close reading in order to solve the mystery.

This genre spreads across many areas of study including history, science, and math. Exploring these topics through mysteries is a great way to engage readers in another area of interest. Reading mysteries relies on looking for patterns and decoding clues that help in learning math skills.

Whether readers are reading the books independently or you are reading with them, engaging with them after they have read the book is still important. We've included several activities at the end of each book to make this both fun and educational.

Do you think you and your reader have what it takes to be a detective? Can you solve the mystery? Will you accept the challenge?

Rourke Educational Media

Table of Contents

The Not-So-Great Surprise

"Surprise!" Miss Flores announced on Monday morning when I entered room 113, home of the best third grade class at Watson Elementary. Only, it wasn't really a surprise at all. Not if surprises are supposed to be fun, anyway.

I dropped my backpack on the floor and threw my arms up toward the ceiling. "Miss Flores, what in the world happened in here?"

My best friend Ronald "Rocket" Gonzaga came in behind me. "Did aliens attack our classroom?"

Miss Flores laughed, even though we weren't even joking. "Not quite. I decided to rearrange the room. What do you think?"

"This is on purpose?" Lyra Ladsen groaned.

For almost the whole year our desks had been clustered together in groups of five. My name is Caleb James, and my best friends Rocket, Lyra,

Tully, Alex, and I all got to sit together. We didn't just talk, tell jokes, and crack each other up, though. We also solved mysteries all over school. We're known as the Gumshoe Gang. And just in case you're wondering, our shoes are not made of gum.

But now everything was different. Instead of groups, all the desks were in rows. I'd already figured out the math: there was no way we could all be together.

"It's spring!" Miss Flores said happily, clapping her hands. "Change is refreshing!"

Rocket and I raised our eyebrows at each other. We didn't want to disappoint Miss Flores, who was probably the best teacher on the planet. And the prettiest. But don't tell anyone I said so.

I picked up my backpack, only I'd forgotten to zip it up completely, and a whole bunch of stuff spilled out all over the floor: an empty water bottle, several Hot Wheels cars, crumpled up homework assignments, Tootsie Roll wrappers, and a *Hobby Cars Weekly* magazine. A roll of duct tape wobbled underneath the desk where Tully Warren was sitting in the back row.

Tully picked up the tape and handed it to me. Tully is very fashionable for a detective, and she is so smart she does extra homework just for fun. "What do you need this for?"

"My remote controller for my SuperZoom RC car lost the cover for the batteries, so I have to keep taping it up."

"Your controller lost it, or you did?" Alex Price asked as he helped me shove all my stuff back in my backpack. Alex was smart too. He was probably going to be a world famous scientist when he grew up.

"All I know is, it sure wasn't me!" We got most everything back in my bag except for maybe a few candy wrappers and crumpled up papers.

Rocket grabbed my arm. "Where are you sitting? I'm right in the front. Miss Flores must really like me." Rocket got his name from being so fast. He can outrun almost anybody. He is also a jokester, same as me.

"I'm looking for my desk," I said.

"It's not like it's hard to find!" Lyra said loudly. She is loud almost all the time, but that works out for her because she's also the best singer in probably the whole school.

"Where is it?"

"Right there!" Lyra rolled her eyes and pointed at a desk in the front row all the way on the end. The desk had a few scratched-off stickers and pen marks on the top. The cubby was bursting with books, papers, pencils, markers, and bent up paper airplanes. Yep, it was definitely mine.

I unloaded my math, reading, and science books from my backpack. But they wouldn't fit in my cubby (pretty much nothing did anymore), so I had to shove them under my desk. Then I plopped down in my seat and turned to my new neighbor.

And groaned.

Because my new neighbor was none other than Ian Summerhill, my arch nemesis! He was the only other kid almost as obsessed with cars as me. If I read *Hobby Cars Weekly*, so did Ian. If I raced my cars down the slide during recess, so did Ian. And when I customized my special edition ScreamLiner roadster with permanent markers, the next day Ian brought in his own colored car. And on top of all that, Ian the Awful was stinky with a capital P.U.!

Something poked my back. I turned around. Alex sat right behind me. "Hey, this is pretty close, right?"

I pulled my eyelids up with my fingers and stuck my tongue out at him to show that I was glad about that. "I've got a joke for you. What part of a car is the laziest?"

Alex shrugged. "I give up."

"The wheels, because they're always tired!"

We cracked up laughing just as the bell rang. Mrs. Flores cleared her throat and gave us one of her time-to-be-quiet-or-else looks. "Good morning, class. Before we head over to the learning rug, we need to make our food assignments for the spring picnic this Sunday. Our class is in charge of fruit, so let's decide who will bring which fruit, and I'll send a flier home with each of you at the end of the day."

Some kids started telling Miss Flores how they wanted to bring watermelon or raspberries or cantaloupes, but I was already dreaming about the spring picnic, and not the food part of it. Other schools had regular picnics with a lot of sitting around, eating some stuff, and maybe a grownup softball game. But at Watson Elementary, we did our spring picnic the right way.

We played games all afternoon, but not just any games. They were weird, silly games and the grownups and the kids all competed together. There were sack races, pie eating contests, hula hoop challenges, tug of war, and miniature golf that you played with your feet instead of clubs, and a leap frog race, only with real frogs! The principal Mrs. Holmes even let us throw pies at her to raise money for charity. It was pretty hilarious.

But the best part of the spring picnic was the annual RC car championship. Mr. Sleuth and the fourth grade teacher Mr. Z created an obstacle course for remote controlled cars out of orange cones. They put down PVC pipes for hurdles and built ramps out of plywood. Anyone could enter their RC car and race for a golden trophy and money prizes.

Last year, I came in fourth place. You know who came in third, one measly spot in front of me? Ian the Awful, that's who. And he reminded me of it every chance he could.

For months I'd been practicing in my yard

and in my house (don't tell Mom). This year, I was aiming for first place. I even brought my very special SuperZoom 3000 RC car to school a few weeks ago, just to make sure I was getting in as much practice as possible. SuperZoom is a sleek little blue race car with yellow lightning bolts painted on the sides.

"Ahem."

I looked up to see Miss Flores standing in front of my desk. Just then I noticed the other kids were already sitting criss-cross applesauce on the brown learning rug. Oops.

"Too much daydreaming, not enough listening," Miss Flores said gently. "Put your backpack away please, and then join the class."

I lugged my backpack out to my locker in the hallway. It was pretty much an ordeal to squeeze anything in there these days. I had to step on a pile of papers and my blue striped sweatshirt just to get to it.

And that's when I realized it. My SuperZoom RC car, my favorite thing in the whole universe, which was supposed to be safe inside my locker— it wasn't there. My heart dropped all the way down to the toes of my unlaced sneakers. I rummaged frantically through the mountain of books and markers and papers and dirty socks. How could this be? I'd left it right there on Friday. Hadn't I?

The Search for SuperZoom

I could barely stay in my seat through math and reading, even though they were my favorite subjects. During science, Miss Flores talked about the healthy habits of healthy bodies, but I couldn't pay attention. My mind was stuck like glue to thoughts of SuperZoom 3000. What was I going to do if I couldn't find it in time for the spring picnic?

As soon as Miss Flores announced first recess, I bolted out of my seat. I found my friends and told them about my missing car. Tully sighed and shook her head. "I'm sure you'll find it somewhere."

"But it was in my locker—and now it isn't!"

"It's so messy in there, how would you even know?" Alex said.

"Because I checked super carefully!"

"Then let's find it," Rocket said as we walked outside.

Miss Flores was right. Spring was here. Pink and white flowers bloomed all over the place. The sky was deep blue, and the clouds looked like giant cotton balls.

Lyra, Tully, and I climbed onto the tire swing. Rocket and Alex pushed us. "Okay, fine," Lyra said. "I'll help too. Where did you play with it?"

"The cafeteria, the lobby, the playground, and the library."

Tully frowned at me. "The library? Seriously?"

"Why not? The bookcases make a great obstacle course."

We took a few more turns on the tire swing, and then we searched the playground. It wasn't anywhere, not even tucked underneath the slide. I asked Miss Flores if we could look inside the school. She said yes, but we only had 18 minutes, and we couldn't do any running or yelling.

We headed downstairs to the cafeteria, where Mrs. Pumpernickel the lunch lady was hard at work making sloppy joes. She looked a little silly with her white hair all stuffed inside her hairnet. She must not have been feeling very silly though, because she glared at me as she wiped her hands on her apron. "What do you kids want?"

When I asked if she'd seen my RC car, she made a kind of choking noise like my cat Stinkypants Magoo does when he's coughing up a hairball. "You should hope I haven't, young man. If I ever see that troublemaker car again, I'll toss it in my soup pot and cook it up for lunch."

That's when I recalled how Mrs. Pumpernickel wasn't so pleased when SuperZoom went whizzing around the cafeteria, rocketing around tables and chairs and knocking several kids right on their bottoms.

She'd sent me straight to Mrs. Holmes' office. Mrs. Holmes turned the Holmes Eye on me, which was like a terrible laser that could see all the bad stuff you'd done before you even admitted it. That was how SuperZoom got banished to my locker.

I cleared my throat. "So, um, that's a no?"

I'm not sure if the steam was from the sloppy joes frying or if it was coming out of Mrs. Pumpernickel's ears, but either way it was time to go.

"Um, Mrs. Pumpernickel?" Rocket asked, scrunching up his face. "What's that net on your head for? Is it for catching flies?"

That's when Mrs. Pumpernickel started waving her spatula around and sputtering words I didn't even understand.

I yanked on Rocket's arm. We dashed out of there, yelling, "Sorry!" and "Thank you!" from a safe distance.

We nearly ran straight into Mr. Doyle the custodian. He was mopping the hall outside the cafeteria. Rocket's feet slipped on the sudsy floor and his legs slid right out from under him. Oof! He fell flat on his butt.

Mr. Doyle had a concerned look on his face until Rocket and I busted up laughing. Then he scowled. Mr. Doyle is kind of a grouchy guy. Rocket thinks it's because his head is as bald as a balloon. I'm sure it's because he's so busy thinking about stuff he wants to clean that he forgets to have a sense of humor.

"No running!" he growled.

"Sorry!" I gulped. "Have you seen a little blue RC car?"

"Not sure I'd tell you if I did!" Mr. Doyle grumbled. Then he threatened to scrub us with his mop if we didn't scram right out of there. I wasn't a fan of baths anyway, so we race-walked up the stairs toward the library.

The library is a great big room with rows and rows of bookshelves all the way up to the ceiling. Mr. Hornswoggle the librarian loves animals almost as much as he loves books, so the library has a bunch of furry animals in glass cages lined up beneath the windows. My favorite is Fluffy the tarantula, who is as big as a grownup's entire hand.

Mr. Hornswoggle looked up from his desk

when we came in. He patted his vest and took out his glasses. "Eh? Is it time for the third graders already?"

"Not yet," I said. I explained about my missing car.

Mr. Hornswoggle stroked his chin. "Last time I saw it was a few days ago, when I nearly stepped on it as I was climbing down off my stepstool."

I felt my ears getting hot. "Oops."

"I do have something for you, though," Mr. Hornswoggle said, shuffling papers around on his desk. He picked up a yellow slip and handed it to me. "Here it is. A fine for $13.13. I believe your book *RC Racing for Geniuses* is seven weeks overdue."

Tully elbowed me, but all I could do was shrug. It was probably at home someplace, buried underneath my bed or stuffed in my underwear drawer. "I'll find it, sir," I said.

I looked at the clock above Mr. Hornswoggle's desk. Only two minutes left of recess. We waved goodbye and headed back to room 113.

"Your car must be at your house," Alex said.

"Exactly," Lyra said. "It's probably cuddled up

right next to that racing genius book."

"It is not," I said.

Alex let out a sigh. "I think you'd lose your head if it wasn't attached to your neck."

Everybody laughed but me. "Oh yeah? Well, people who wear glass slippers shouldn't kick stones!"

Alex was not even that funny. Suddenly I was sort of glad I was sitting away from my friends. They were acting like big slimy boogers.

I stomped back to my seat. When I went to sit down, I saw a folded up piece of paper on my desk.

I opened it up and read it. My eyeballs just about fell out of my head. I am not even joking.

It was a ransom note. SuperZoom wasn't lost after all. It was stolen!

Ransom Riddler

At lunchtime, we all sat together in the cafeteria. I knew I couldn't stay mad at the rest of the Gumshoe Gang. I needed their help. After all, once the toothpaste is out of the tube, it's too late to close the barn door. I wasn't totally sure what that meant, but it sounded good.

Rocket, Lyra, and I got hot lunches—sloppy joe sandwiches, tater tots, and carrots. I took a giant bite of my sandwich and waved the letter at my friends. "See, I told you!" I sputtered, little bits of meaty sauce dribbling down my chin.

"Gross!" Lyra squealed, covering her eyes.

Sheesh. Didn't she know this was no time for manners? I swallowed a big glob of bread. "Look!"

We read the ransom note together:

By now you may be missing
A certain treasure you've neglected.
To ensure its safekeeping,
A problem must be corrected.

Many tales you may spin
When you follow the right clues
Letters are aplenty,
But only if you pay your dues.

If this precious treasure
You wish to save,
Look for the face that does not frown
With the hands that do not wave.

But be nimble, and be quick
or the Rc Race you'll have to skip.

"Holy Moly!" Lyra exclaimed.

"How interesting!" Alex said.

"No, not interesting!" I cried. "I need my SuperZoom back before the championship race!"

"We'll get it back," Tully said. She was already pulling out her notebook. From where, I have no idea. She was tricky like that. Tully was in charge of writing down all the notes for the Gumshoe Gang's cases, like suspects, alibis, and clues. The notebook had yellow polka-dots with REAL DETECTIVE CLUES: PRIVATE: NO PEEKING scrawled in purple marker across the front and THAT MEANS YOU! written at the bottom.

"We should make a list of suspects," Alex said. "Just like a regular case."

Tully nodded as she nibbled on a carrot. "And in the meantime, we do what the ransom says."

"But they aren't even asking for money!"

"The word 'dues' could mean money," Alex said. "Maybe there'll be another note that tells you how much to pay. Maybe the riddle will lead us to it."

I nodded, taking deep breaths. That made sense.

"So who would want to take SuperZoom?"

"Like, everybody!" Rocket said with a giggle.

I glared at him. "Not everybody. Ian the Awful should be first on the list. He is the worst! He wants to win the competition almost as much as me."

"Mrs. Pumpernickel was not exactly happy to see you," Lyra said. "She threatened to turn SuperZoom to soup."

"And she was not even joking!" I said. "She should be number one on the list too."

"Come to think of it," Alex said, pushing up his

glasses, "Mr. Doyle wasn't too fond of your car either. Or Mr. Hornswoggle. And what about all the kids you knocked down in the cafeteria?"

"Slow down," Tully said, writing furiously.

"Make everybody number one on the list!" Rocket yelled.

I socked him in the arm. "That is not helpful."

He smacked me back. "How's that?"

"Guys!" Tully said sternly, just as the bell rang. "Quick. Anybody else?"

"Yes! My little sister, Ella."

"What? She's like five years old!" Lyra gathered up everybody's trash as we stood up.

"She is five years old," I said. "But she's been out to get me since the day she was born."

Next we had art with Mrs. Center, who is so talented that she teaches art and music. We worked on posters for the spring picnic to put up around the school. I couldn't find all of my colored pencils, but Lyra shared hers. I drew a picture of the championship obstacle course, with SuperZoom 3000 breaking across the finish line. Ian the Awful's green monster truck Bone Crusher was a very distant last place. The more I colored, the more I felt like angry bees were buzzing around inside my head.

"Look Ian," I said, holding up my poster. "Here's a picture of how I'm going to beat you, just as soon as I get my car back that you stole!"

"I didn't steal your stupid car!" Ian shouted. "I can beat you just fine without cheating!"

"That's enough!" Mrs. Center said sharply. She folded her arms across her front like she did when she'd lost her patience and didn't feel like looking for it.

"Ian the Awful stole my SuperZoom on Friday and now he's sending me ransom notes!" I hollered.

"That's not true!" Ian shot back.

"Boys! Calm down or I'll have to send you both to Mrs. Holmes. Do you have any evidence for your accusation, Caleb?"

"Only my excellent detective skill of sniffing out stinky liars!"

Ian turned to Mrs. Center. "I wasn't even at school on Friday! I went home sick with a stomachache before first recess. You can ask the school nurse. So I couldn't have done it!"

Oops. Actually, now I kind of remembered that. I slumped down in my seat. "Okay, fine. But I bet he wanted to."

Mrs. Center gave me one of her worst I'm-very-disappointed-in-you-young-man faces.

Okay, so he didn't steal SuperZoom. Ian was still awful. And sneaky. And, he smelled like stinky armpits. From now on, I was going to watch everything he did with a fine-tuned comb!

Riddle Me This

I spent the whole rest of the day trying to figure out the ransom riddle, but I couldn't quite put my thumb on it. After school, I got to stay at extended day with Alex since Mom was gone on a business trip all week. Dad couldn't get me and Ella until his accounting office was finished at five o'clock.

We still weren't able to figure it out, mostly because Ella kept being a giant pest by jumping on us, pulling on our clothes, and trying to braid our hair. And Alex doesn't even have hair!

By the time we got to Tuesday morning recess, I was really hoping the rest of the Gumshoe Gang had some good ideas. And luckily for me, they did. We sat in our favorite spot under the slide. Tully studied the ransom note with her magnifying glass covered in pink diamonds.

"Look for the face that doesn't frown," Lyra

said. "So that could be somebody who smiles all the time. Miss Flores is super smiley. So is Mrs. Center."

"But nobody smiles all the time," Alex said. "What if it means the face of an animal? What class pets do we have?"

I ticked them off on my fingers. "In our room, there's the goldfish, then in fourth grade there's Spike the lizard, and fifth grade has Muffy the bunny and Samson the mouse. Mr. Hornswoggle has Zake the Snake, Howard the Hamster, Fluffy the Tarantula, and CoCo the turtle."

"I don't think animals smile or frown," Tully said. "And besides, none of them have hands. What else has hands?"

"Aliens!" Rocket cried.

"Gloves!" Lyra said.

"Monkeys!" I said.

"Okay, good guesses. But how is a monkey or an alien going to lead us to the next clue?" Tully tapped her chin with her unicorn pencil. "Ugh. This stinks. And it's almost time to go already!"

I looked around for a clock, forgetting for a second that there were no clocks outside. Then

I had an idea so fantastic it was like a lightbulb flicked on right over my head. "Aha! I've got it! A clock has a face but doesn't frown, and it has hands that don't wave—a minute hand and a second hand!"

Lyra high-fived me. "But are we going to have to check every single clock in the whole school? That will take practically forever!"

Miss Flores blew her whistle. Tully tucked the ransom note inside her notebook. "We'll figure out the rest at lunch. But check out every clock we see."

On the way back to Room 113, we examined Mr. Sleuth's clock in his secretary office, the lobby clock, the two gymnasium clocks covered in wire cages, and the clock with flowers instead of numbers in our own classroom. Not a ransom note in sight.

Ian the Awful and I ignored each other during language arts and spelling. But out of the corner of my eye, I was watching him like he was a hawk. I also had to try not to breathe at him either, since he smelled like stinky socks.

At lunchtime, Alex wanted to interview Mrs.

Pumpernickel, since she was at the top of our suspects list. "I think it's best you stay here," Tully said when I stood up to go with them. "Mrs. Pumpernickel is not your number one fan. Yours either, Rocket."

So Rocket and I sat at our table dipping droopy French fries in a glob of mayonnaise. I missed Mom's lunches. She always cut my peanut butter and honey sandwiches into hearts.

Rocket poked me. "Give me a joke."

"Okay. What happens when a frog's car breaks down?"

Rocket shook his head.

"It gets toad away!"

We cracked up. Rocket could always help me feel better.

When the gang returned, Tully shook her head at us. "Mrs. Pumpernickel's assistant, Mr. Colby, confirmed that Mrs. Pumpernickel was in the cafeteria kitchen from 9 a.m. until after all the lunches were served. She couldn't have left the ransom note."

"Back to square two," I said with a sigh.

Tully narrowed her eyes. "I was thinking

about the second verse: 'spinning tales,' 'letters of plenty,' 'following clues,' and 'paying your dues.' 'Tales' is spelled like stories, not like animal tails."

"And letters could mean alphabet letters," Lyra said slowly. "Letters make up words and sentences, which make stories."

Alex nodded. "That makes sense so far."

"And what if 'dues' doesn't mean the ransom money?" I asked.

Alex pushed on his glasses. "Dues could be something you owe."

"Like my $13.13 overdue book fine?"

"Yes!" Tully exclaimed. "Stories, letters, and dues can all be found at the library! Mr. Hornswoggle is still a suspect!"

"And he has a clock on his desk!" I said.

"But we don't have library until tomorrow afternoon," Rocket said.

"We have ten minutes left of lunch. Let's get a hall pass!" I leapt out of my seat. We threw away our trash, asked for the hall pass, and hurried to the library.

When we examined Mr. Hornswoggle's clock, we found a folded up piece of paper taped

underneath it. "Aha!" I shouted.

Mr. Hornswoggle squinted at us as he polished his spectacles with his vest. "Eh? How'd that get there?"

"It's a ransom note, sir," Tully said. "May I ask your whereabouts yesterday morning?"

"Well, let me think. You came to see me at about 10:15 a.m., I believe. I'd just gotten back from an optometrist appointment to get new glasses. I even have the receipt right here on my desk," he said, showing it to us.

Sheesh. Suspects were dropping like mosquitoes around here. "You are cleared of all suspicion," I said.

"Well, that's a relief, I suppose." As we waved goodbye, he called out, "Don't forget to return that book, Caleb!"

After lunch on Tuesdays, we had computer lab upstairs. We paused outside the door to read the newest ransom note. It was another riddle:

If finding your treasure is your wish,
Hunt for the net which catches no fish.
Find what barks but does not speak
If your treasure you want to keep.

"Ugh," Rocket moaned. "These are so hard! Fish don't bark . . . do they?"

"The only animals that bark are dogs and seals," Tully said.

"Atten-SHUN!" Mr. Benton bellowed, which meant it was time to get in our seats lickety-split. Lucky for me, Rocket sat next to me in this class.

"I think I know this one," I whispered. "Trees have bark."

"But no bite!" Rocket giggled, then clapped his hand over his mouth. Mr. Benton was across the room helping Javier and didn't notice.

"That means the net has to be outside somewhere. Find the net, then find the closest tree."

"How about Mrs. Pumpernickel's hairnet?"

We cracked up over that. "It has to be outside!"

"Oh fine. What about the net on a basketball hoop? There's no fish in there!"

My heart jumped in my chest like a kangaroo. "Yes! That's it!"

"Boys!" Mr. Benton said sternly.

We paid attention the whole rest of computer labs, only making silly faces at each other a couple of times. It wasn't terribly hard because we'd already figured out the next clue. There was a huge maple tree right next to the basketball courts. And second recess was next!

chapter 5

Riddle Me That

As soon as the bell rang for recess, we raced out to the playground. I explained the answer to the riddle to Tully and Alex, who'd also figured it out already. Grr. Why'd they have to be such smarty-pants all the time?

We went straight to the big maple tree. We ran our hands all over the trunk and the roots, searching for the next clue. Alex cupped his hands together and boosted Rocket up so he could feel inside an old bird's nest on a branch just above our heads. "Eureka!" he cried.

He dropped to the ground, and we crowded in to read the next clue:

Here you must enter,
Though you may not come in
Where there is space but no room,
This is how you begin.
Find the keys, which open no door,
or your treasure you ll see no more.

"Well, that sounds troubling," Tully said with a frown.

"We're up a tree without a paddle!" I cried. I felt like a little kid whose ice cream cone just went splat all over the floor. "He just said I'll never see SuperZoom again! The Ransom Riddler is never gonna give it back!"

"Oooh, Ransom Riddler is a great bad-guy name!" Rocket said. He sounded way too happy.

"We'll get it back," Lyra said, patting my shoulder. "We just have to solve all the riddles."

"Lyra's right," Tully said. "Let's talk this out."

I sucked in my cheeks. I tried to make my brain think really hard, but the parts of the riddle were all scrambled up like pieces of a jigsaw puzzle. "Whoever heard of entering but not going in? And keys that don't open locked doors?"

"And why are rocks heavier than feathers?" Rocket asked.

I glared at him. "That is not even what we're talking about right now."

"Wait a minute!" Lyra nearly shouted. She started dancing around like there were ants all in her pants. "Woohoo! I know this one!"

"Then hurry up and say it!"

"What has keys besides locks?"

We stared at her blankly. "We don't know," I said. "That's why you're supposed to tell us."

"A piano!"

"Of course!" Tully said. "But what about all the space and entering stuff?"

Lyra scrunched up her face. "Well, when you lift up the piano lid, there's lots of space but you can't actually go inside it 'cause there isn't room."

"That's good enough for me!" I cried. "Let's go to the music room right now. I can see the carrot at the end of the tunnel!"

Miss Flores gave us the hall pass, and we hurried inside. The art and music room door was open. Tully knocked as we entered.

"Well, welcome back." Mrs. Center was playing the piano, which reminded me of a good joke.

"Mrs. Center, did you know you can tune a piano, but you can't tuna fish? Get it? Tune a fish?" Rocket and I elbowed each other and cracked up.

Mrs. Center raised her eyebrows at us. "I love tuna fish!"

"Can we check your piano?" Tully showed her the ransom riddle.

"That is an interesting riddle, indeed." Mrs. Center helped us lift the lid of the piano. Inside the piano were all kinds of wires that connected to the piano keys. It was super awesome looking, but there was no ransom note. We looked around and under and on top of the piano. Nothing.

"Oh," I said softly, "that puts a monkey in the wrench." I felt like my heart was just run over by a monster truck. One that was little, and green, and remote controlled.

"Now what?" Rocket moaned.

"Keep working at it," Mrs. Center said gently. "All great quests are worth the effort."

"We got it wrong the first time, that's all," Tully said.

The only problem was no matter how much we kept working at it and reading it and reading it again, we couldn't solve it. The rest of Wednesday passed by without any new ideas from anybody, not even alien ones from Rocket.

My insides were getting so twisted up that I could barely eat. When Dad made my favorite macaroni and cheese for supper, it just looked like bright orange mush. Even my little sister Ella tried to cheer me up by covering my backpack in glittery princess stickers. But nothing helped.

I was used to misplacing stuff and losing things for a little while, but I'd never missed anything so badly as my RC race car. What if I never got SuperZoom back? I mean, not just for the big spring picnic race, but never ever?

Ransom Blues

On Thursday, I thought about the ransom riddle all through both recesses, lunch, computer lab, and my other classes too. Ian the Awful kept making nasty faces at me. I wanted to do something mean right back like throw a moldy banana peel at him. I mean, he even kind of smelled like a moldy banana peel.

And then just like that, the last bell rang. We only had one day left to catch the Ransom Riddler and get SuperZoom back before the spring picnic!

During extended day, I sat at a table with Alex. We were supposed to be working on our Healthy Bodies: Personal Hygiene worksheets, but I couldn't seem to remember how long we ought to brush our teeth for (ten seconds?) or how often we were supposed to change our underwear (once a month?).

My little sister Ella squirmed and wiggled around next to me while she colored a bunch of dots on yellow construction paper. She was singing some sort of nonsense words to herself. "What are you doing?" Alex asked her.

"I'm practicing my Spanishing!" she said proudly.

"Well, I like your pigtails."

Ella scrunched up her face in horror. "I don't have pig's tails! These are my tails!"

Alex and I raised our eyebrows at each other. "Good to know," I said.

Alex wrote down a list of all the important words in the latest riddle: enter, come in, space, room, begin, keys, door. He drew arrows and circles around the words. He wrote them forward and backward. "Still nothing," he groaned.

Ella started tapping the dots on her paper. She made clicking sounds with her tongue.

"Now what are you doing?" I asked her.

"I'm computering a story!"

"What's your story about?" Alex asked.

"I don't know, dude. I can't read yet!"

Alex and I chuckled. I pointed to the dots on

her paper. "But what are those?"

Ella grinned. "I'm computering the buttons."

"Computers don't have buttons. They're called keys."

And that's when I smacked my own forehead. "That's it! Computer keys!"

"Yes!" Alex blurted. "That's what 'you must enter but not come in' means—the 'enter' key on the keyboard! Same with 'space but no room'—the space bar!"

"We need to go to the computer lab!"

"Me too!" Ella yelled, bouncing right out of her seat.

"Oh, all right. Come on!"

We got a hall pass from the extended day teacher and made it all the way across the school and upstairs to the computer lab as fast as we could with a little sister tagging along. We were just in time too, because Mr. Benton was about to lock the door.

"Can we look at all the computers?" I asked, panting for air.

"You guys sound out of breath."

"No sir," chirped Ella. "We have more."

Mr. Benton laughed as he let us in. "There's a broken computer over in the corner. If someone was going to leave a note in here, that's probably a good place."

Sure enough, there it was, taped to the keyboard. I wanted to smack my own head again. "We were in here today, using the computers, and we didn't even think of it!"

"All detectives have bad days sometimes. But look, I think this is the last clue." I looked over Alex's shoulder as he unfolded the ransom:

If you want your treasure returned,
First this lesson you must have learned
clean up your things
This is what consideration means.
You might just be surprised
Happiness for all is what it brings.
When prepared you think you are
come see the prince
come find a pal.
Here will be your treasured car.

I took a deep breath. The truth hit me right between the nose. This time, I knew what the Ransom Riddler meant. And I knew exactly what I needed to do. It was time for me to wake up and listen to the music.

I asked Alex to take Ella back to extended day. I had work to do.

The Carrot at the End of the Tunnel

The next morning when I got to school, I felt lighter than a feather floating around in a bright blue sky. I opened my locker and hung up my sweater and backpack. There was actually an amazing amount of room in that thing.

I slid my homework folder into my cubby and sat down at my desk. All my pencils, pens, markers, and paper were right where I needed them. The top of my desk was scrubbed squeaky clean.

Funny story: it turned out the rotten eggs stench I thought was coming from Ian the Awful was actually a half-rotten bologna sandwich all squished up in the back corner of my desk cubby. I really wish I was joking about that.

Lyra, Rocket, and Tully came up to my desk and stood there with their mouths hanging open.

Tully's eyes were big as SuperZoom's hubcaps.

"Oh wow! Everything's so . . . clean!"

Rocket leaned in close to my face and squinted at me. "Where is the real Caleb James? What have you done with him, you alien imposter!!"

"Okay, class! Back to your seats please!" Miss Flores gave me such a huge smile I thought she might get cracks in her cheeks.

I turned real quick to Ian. "I'm sorry I was so mean, even after I knew you weren't the Ransom Riddler. Also, I was the stinky one, not you."

Ian kept staring straight ahead. A minute later, he reached over and put an awesome red Camaro Hot Wheels car on my desk. Also keeping my eyes straight ahead, I reached in my cubby and put a yellow Mustang on his desk. "Hot Wheels are the Wheel Deal," I said.

"You auto know," he whispered back.

We cracked up. And that's how I knew we were going to be friends, after all.

chapter 8

Unmasking the Ransom Riddler

When it was finally time for first recess, I didn't even have to ask Miss Flores for a hall pass; she just plopped it right on my nice clean desk. Of course, the rest of the Gumshoe Gang couldn't wait to come too.

"So who's the Ransom Riddler?" Tully flipped through her notebook as we trotted toward Mrs. Holmes' office. I knew that's where we needed to go by combining the "prince" and "pal" words in the last riddle. "I can't believe we haven't figured it out!"

I shrugged. "It doesn't even matter as long as I get my RC car back!"

"It matters to me," Tully grumbled.

"Come right in," Mr. Sleuth said to us. He did a sort of bow and winked at me as we walked into the office.

Mrs. Holmes was sitting in her leather

principal's chair. SuperZoom 3000 was sitting right on her desk! And there was someone else standing next to Mrs. Holmes.

"Mr. Doyle!" I gasped.

"It was you all along?" Tully asked, dismayed. "But you said you hadn't seen the car!"

Mr. Doyle grunted. "If you detectives were paying attention like you're supposed to, you would have noticed that I said, 'Not sure I'd tell you if I did', which was not a confirmation either way."

Tully swallowed. "Oh."

"But why'd you do it?" Alex asked.

Mr. Doyle nodded in my direction. "Because I was tired of cleaning up after Caleb. He is always leaving cars, trash, clothes, airplanes and whatnot everywhere. It's a lot of extra work for me. Then last Friday I saw that his locker was so full, his stuff was all over the floor—including that race car that's so special to him."

Oops. My face got all hot and prickly. I hung my head. "I am really sorry. I guess I didn't think about my messiness being a problem for other people."

"Well." Mr. Doyle grunted again. "I had the

idea to do something fun, and maybe teach you a bit of a lesson at the same time."

I jerked my head back up. I couldn't believe what I'd just heard. "You wanted to do something—fun?"

Mrs. Holmes snorted. "Believe it or not, Caleb, Mr. Doyle has a terrific sense of humor."

That was about the craziest thing I'd ever heard, but I kept that thought to myself. I was also thinking something else kind of crazy. "Did you already know Mr. Doyle took my car? Is that why none of the grownups acted upset?"

Mrs. Holmes nodded. "Yes, everyone was in on it. Even your dad."

Wow. It was gonna take a while to wrap myself around that one. I looked longingly at SuperZoom.

"Oh, go ahead and take it," Mrs. Holmes said, laughing. "But don't even think about driving it on school grounds—not until Sunday, at least!"

"Thank you!" I didn't need to be told twice. I grabbed my car, and we skedaddled right out of that place.

"You guys go back to recess," I said, grinning at my friends. "I have a book to return to the library."

Sunday finally arrived. The spring picnic was even more amazing than I'd imagined. Mom was back from her trip, and we competed in the sack race and the egg toss together. Mom got egg all over her face! Ella jumped around in the bounce house until she couldn't stand up anymore. Rocket and I threw pies at Mr. Benton and Mr. Sleuth. It was great.

And then it was time for the big RC Obstacle Course Championship. Everybody watched along the sidelines and cheered the racers. There were 20 cars and trucks of all different shapes and sizes. SuperZoom raced like a champ, streaking around the track like blue lightning!

SuperZoom came in second place. Ian's Bone Crusher monster truck came in third. And you know who came in first? Mrs. Holmes, that's who! I did not even know she liked RC cars. How funny is that?

Q & A with Author Kyla Steinkraus

How did you come up with the story for the Ransom Riddler?

As a writer, I need to use my imagination to build my stories, to create characters and have fun and interesting things happen to them. To come up with ideas, I like to play the "What If?" game. What if a student was so messy that he created a whole bunch of hassles for other people? What if one of those people was the custodian? What if the custodian decided to play a trick on the student and hopefully help him learn a lesson at the same time? And that is the beginning of a mystery!

How do you get your ideas for your characters?

I have a son who is in third grade. He loves RC cars. He also happens to have a little problem with messiness. I take a few characteristics from a real person and add other things to make an imaginary character.

Did you come up with the ransom riddles yourself?

Yes I did! It can be hard work to create your own riddles, but it is fun and worth it in the end.

Discussion Questions

1. Why don't Ian and Caleb like each other?
2. Tully makes a long list of suspects. How many can you remember? What motive did each of them have to want to take Caleb's car?
3. What does Caleb do in the end to earn SuperZoom back?
4. How do Caleb and Ian end up being friends? Does that surprise you?
5. What lesson do you think that Caleb learned in the end?

Vocabulary

Write each word on an index card. Then write each definition on a separate index card. Mix them up and lay them face down on the table. Take turns selecting two cards. If you select the word and its definition, you get a match. The person with the most matches at the end of the game wins!

banish: to send someone or something away permanently

blurt: to say something suddenly, without thinking

consideration: to show you care about other people's needs and feelings

frantic: wildly excited or fearful

holler: to yell loudly

neglect: to fail to do something from carelessness

ransom: money that is demanded before someone or something held captive will be released

riddle: a question that seems to make no sense but has a clever answer

scrunch: to make wrinkles or creases in a smooth surface

wobble: to move unsteadily from side to side

Writing Prompt

Write your own riddle! The riddle can rhyme, but it doesn't have to. Pick an object or place for your answer. What does it look like? Sound like? Taste like? Smell like? Feel like? How is it used? What does it do? Imagine you are the answer to the riddle. How would you describe yourself? Write three or four clues and share your riddle!

Websites to Visit

www.abcya.com/create_and_build_car.htm

http://kids.niehs.nih.gov/games/riddles/
not_so_hard_rd1.htm

http://kids.mysterynet.com/

About the Author

Kyla Steinkraus loves mysteries and third graders (she happens to have one at home), so writing books for this series was a perfect fit. She and her two awesome kids love to  snuggle up and read good books together. Kyla also loves playing games, laughing at funny jokes, and eating anything with chocolate in it.

About the Illustrator

I have always loved drawing from a very young age. While I was at school, most of my time was spent drawing comics and copying my favorite characters.  With a portfolio under my arm, I started drawing comics for newspapers and fanzines. After I finished my studies I decided to try to make a living as a freelance illustrator... and here I am!